Dear Parent:
Your child's love of reading starts here!

Every child learns to read in a different way and at his or her own speed. Some go back and forth between reading levels and read favorite books again and again. Others read through each level in order. You can help your young reader improve and become more confident by encouraging his or her own interests and abilities. From books your child reads with you to the first books he or she reads alone, there are I Can Read Books for every stage of reading:

SHARED READING
Basic language, word repetition, and whimsical illustrations, ideal for sharing with your emergent reader

BEGINNING READING
Short sentences, familiar words, and simple concepts for children eager to read on their own

READING WITH HELP
Engaging stories, longer sentences, and language play for developing readers

READING ALONE
Complex plots, challenging vocabulary, and high-interest topics for the independent reader

ADVANCED READING
Short paragraphs, chapters, and exciting themes for the perfect bridge to chapter books

I Can Read Books have introduced children to the joy of reading since 1957. Featuring award-winning authors and illustrators and a fabulous cast of beloved characters, I Can Read Books set the standard for beginning readers.

A lifetime of discovery begins with the magical words **"I Can Read!"**

Visit www.icanread.com for information
on enriching your child's reading experience.

I Can Read Book® is a trademark of HarperCollins Publishers.

The Berenstain Bears' Big Machines
Copyright © 2017 by Berenstain Publishing, Inc.
All rights reserved. Manufactured in China.
No part of this book may be used or reproduced in any manner whatsoever without written permission except in the case of brief
quotations embodied in critical articles and reviews. For information address HarperCollins Children's Books, a division of
HarperCollins Publishers, 195 Broadway, New York, NY 10007.
www.icanread.com

Library of Congress Control Number: 2016957945
ISBN 978-0-06-235039-8 (trade bdg.) — ISBN 978-0-06-235038-1 (pbk.)

17 18 19 20 21   SCP   10 9 8 7 6 5 4 3 2 1
❖
First Edition

I Can Read!

BEGINNING READING 1

The Berenstain Bears'®

BIG MACHINES

Mike Berenstain

Based on the characters created by
Stan and Jan Berenstain

HARPER

An Imprint of HarperCollinsPublishers

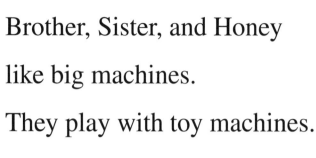

Brother, Sister, and Honey
like big machines.
They play with toy machines.
They make big machine noises.
"Brrm! Brrm! Rowr! Rowr!"

BRRM!

ROWR!

Grizzly Gramps comes by.
"Would you like to see some
real machines?" he asks.
"Yes, we would!" say the cubs.

Gramps takes them to visit
his friend Big Jake.
Big Jake has big machines!

Big Jake is a builder.
His workers are getting
things ready to build.
They dig with a backhoe.
They move dirt around with
a loader and bulldozer.

Front-end loader

Bulldozer

Backhoe

Big Jake shows Gramps

and the cubs around.

"To dig really big holes," he says,

"you need really big diggers!"

Power shovel

Cable power shovel

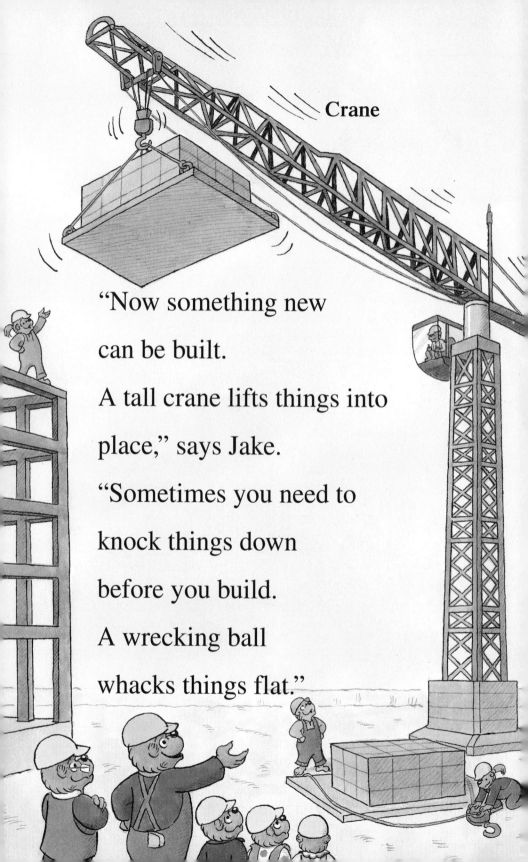

Crane

"Now something new
can be built.
A tall crane lifts things into
place," says Jake.
"Sometimes you need to
knock things down
before you build.
A wrecking ball
whacks things flat."

Wrecking ball

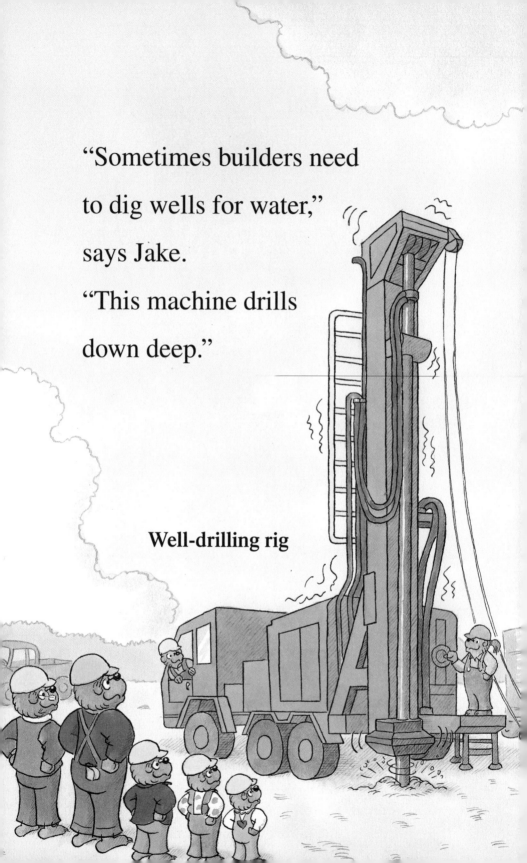

"Sometimes builders need to dig wells for water," says Jake.
"This machine drills down deep."

Well-drilling rig

"Sometimes posts need to go in the ground. This machine pounds them in."

Pile driver

"Come on!" says Big Jake.

"We'll see more machines!

Here, workers are making a road.

First they make the ground flat.

Then they roll out stone.

Then they lay down the road."

Paver

Roller

Road grader

Big Jake drives past a farm.

"Here, tractors do many jobs," says Jake.

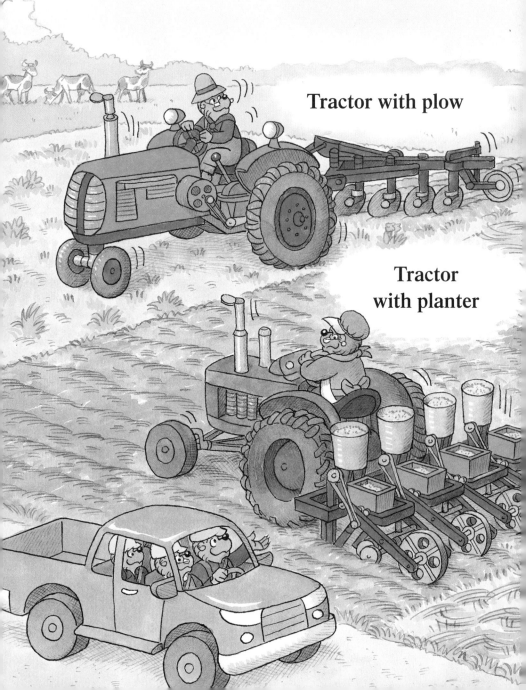

Tractor with plow

Tractor
with planter

"They dig up the earth and plant seeds.

They pull machines to gather hay."

Tractor with rake

**Tractor
with baler**

"To gather wheat," says Jake,

"farmers use very big machines."

**Combine
harvester**

"They cut the wheat and shoot
it into a big wagon."

21

"Some farmers grow trees," says Jake.

"They dig holes to plant them.

Later they dig them up to move them."

Auger

Tree spade

Big Jake drives on.

"Here, in the woods," he says,

"workers cut down trees.

They use special machines.

Some cut and gather tree

trunks.

Others pick them up to move

them around.

The wood will go to build

houses."

Feller
buncher

Logging
skidder

"The biggest big machines are for mining," says Jake. "Here, workers dig into the earth for metal and coal. Metal makes things strong. Coal burns to make things go."

Dragline power shovel

Mining
truck

"Some coal is deep under the earth," says Jake.

"Big machines tunnel into solid rock to get it."

Coal-mining road header

"Here is the biggest machine
of them all!" says Jake.

"It digs up coal that is not too deep."

"Wow!" say the cubs.

"It's ginormous!"

Bucket wheel
excavator

Jake drives Gramps and the cubs
back to where they started.

"So long, Jake!" they call.

"Thanks for the tour!"

"Anytime!" he says.

"For big machines,

just come to me, Big Jake!"